W9-ART-998

READ ME A STORY

A Child's Book of Favorite Tales

The Gingerbread Boy

There was once a little old man and a little old woman who had no children. One day the little old woman said, "I shall make myself a little boy out of gingerbread."

She mixed the dough, kneaded it well, and cut out and shaped a little gingerbread boy. She stuck on two raisins for eyes and three for buttons, and put a smile on his face. Then she popped him in the oven to bake.

When the little old woman opened the oven

door, out jumped the little gingerbread boy. He danced across the kitchen floor, through the open door, and ran off down the street. The little old man and the little old woman chased after him, shouting, "Stop, stop, little gingerbread boy!"

But the little gingerbread boy ran on ahead of them, calling:

"Run, run as fast as you can,
You can't catch me,
I'm the gingerbread man!"

And the little old man and the little old woman couldn't catch him.

The little gingerbread boy ran on until he came to a cow in a meadow. "Stop, stop, little gingerbread boy!" said the cow. "You look good enough to eat."

But the little gingerbread boy ran past the cow, shouting, "I've run away from a little old man and a little old woman. I can run away from you too.

"Run, run, as fast as you can,
You can't catch me,
I'm the gingerbread man!"

And the cow couldn't catch him.

On and on ran the little gingerbread boy. He met a horse taking a drink at a stream.

"Hey, you, stop!" said the horse. "I want to see what you taste like."

But the little gingerbread boy skipped on past the horse, shouting, "I've run away from a little old man, a little old woman and a cow. I can run away from you too.

"Run, run, as fast as you can,
You can't catch me,
I'm the gingerbread man!"

And the horse couldn't catch him.

The little gingerbread boy ran faster and faster. He came to a farmer in a field.

"Stop, little gingerbread boy!" cried the farmer. "I'll have you for my tea."

But the little gingerbread boy just darted between his legs, shouting, "I've run away from a little old man, a little old woman, a cow and a horse. I can run away from you too.

"Run, run, as fast as you can,
You can't catch me,
I'm the gingerbread man!"

The farmer chased him, but the little gingerbread boy was far too quick and the farmer couldn't catch him.

The little gingerbread boy ran on and on until he came to the big wide river. Then he stopped.

Just then a fox came trotting up. The fox thought the little gingerbread boy would make a tasty snack.

He was a clever, cunning fox, so he said, "I'll help you cross the river, little gingerbread boy. Sit on my tail and I'll swim you over to the other side."

And the little gingerbread boy climbed onto the fox's tail, and the fox began to swim across the river.

"You're getting wet," said the fox. "Why don't you jump onto my back?"

So the little gingerbread boy jumped onto the fox's back.

When they were halfway across, the fox said, "You're too heavy to sit on my back. Why don't you jump onto my nose?"

So the little gingerbread boy jumped onto the fox's nose.

When they got to the other side the fox opened his jaws and went SNAP!

"Oh, dear me," said the little gingerbread boy, "I am half gone."

SNAP! went the fox a second time.

"Oh, dear me," said the little gingerbread boy, "I am three-quarters gone."

SNAP! went the fox a third time. And this time, there wasn't anything left at all of the little gingerbread boy.

The Three Little Pigs

Once upon a time there were three little pigs who went out into the world to seek their fortune.

The first little pig set off through the fields. There he met a man carrying a bundle of straw.

"Please, man," said the little pig, "will you give me some straw so that I can build myself a house?"

"As much as you need, little pig," said the man.

The man gave the straw to the little pig, and the little pig built himself a straw house.

In a little while a wolf came along and knocked on the door.

"Little pig, little pig," said the wolf, "let me come in."

"No, no, by the hair of my chinny, chin, chin, I will not let you in," said the little pig.

"Then I'll huff and I'll puff and I'll blow your house down," said the wolf.

And he huffed and he puffed and he blew the house down and ate up the little pig.

The second little pig went up the hill to the woods. There he met a man carrying a bundle of sticks.

"Please, man," said the little pig, "will you give me some sticks so that I can build myself a house?"

"As many as you need, little pig," said the man.

The man gave some sticks to the little pig, and

the little pig built himself a wooden house.

In a little while the wolf came along and knocked on the door.

"Little pig, little pig," said the wolf, "let me come in."

"No, no, by the hair of my chinny, chin, chin, I will not let you in," said the little pig.

"Then I'll huff and I'll puff and I'll blow your house down," snarled the wolf.

And he huffed and he puffed and he blew the house down and ate up the second little pig.

The third little pig skipped down the lane towards the town. On the way he met a man carrying a load of bricks.

"Please, man," said the little pig, "will you give me some bricks so that I can build myself a house?"

"As many as you need, little pig," said the man.

He gave some bricks to the little pig, and the little pig built himself a brick house.

No sooner had the little pig settled into his new home than the wolf came along and knocked at the door.

"Little pig, little pig," said the wolf, "let me come in."

"No, no, by the hair of my chinny, chin, chin, I will not let you in," said the little pig.

"Then I'll huff and I'll puff and I'll blow your house down," roared the wolf.

And he huffed and he puffed, and he huffed and he puffed, but he couldn't blow down the strong little brick house.

Then the wolf was angry. He sprang onto the roof and shouted, "Little pig, I'm coming down the chimney and I'm going to eat you up for my dinner!"

But the little pig was ready for the wolf. He

First she lay down on the great big bed, but it was too hard. Next she lay down on the middle-sized bed, but it was too soft. But when she lay down on the tiny wee bed, it was just right and Goldilocks fell asleep at once.

While she was still sleeping the three bears came back from their walk in the woods. They went over to their bowls of porridge on the kitchen table.

"Who's been eating my porridge?" said Father Bear in his rough, gruff voice.

"Who's been eating my porridge?" said Mother Bear in her soft voice.

"Who's been eating my porridge? It's all gone!" said Baby Bear in his tiny wee voice.

Then the three bears looked at their chairs.

"Who's been sitting on my chair?" said Father Bear in his rough, gruff voice.

"Who's been sitting on my chair?" said Mother Bear in her soft voice.

"Who's been sitting on my chair and broken it all to bits?" said Baby Bear in his tiny wee voice, and he started to cry.

Then the three bears went upstairs to their bedroom.

"Who's been sleeping in my bed?" said Father Bear in his rough, gruff voice.

"Who's been sleeping in my bed?" said Mother Bear in her soft voice.

"Who's sleeping in my bed? She's still there!" said Baby Bear in his tiny wee voice.

Goldilocks woke with a start. As soon as she saw the three bears, she jumped out of bed and ran down the stairs, out of the door, and away into the woods.

And that was the last the three bears ever saw of Goldilocks.

pair of trousers, and knit them some woolen socks."

"And I'll make them some shoes from the very softest leather I can buy," said the shoemaker.

It took hours to cut out and sew such tiny things, but by the next night everything was ready. The shoemaker and his wife laid the clothes and shoes out neatly on the workbench. Then they hid in the corner and waited.

As the clock struck midnight, the elves came running in. They jumped up and down with excitement at the sight of the little coats and trousers, the woolen socks and soft leather shoes, and pulled them on and danced around the room.

Then they ran out of the door, and that was the last that was ever seen of them. But the shoemaker always had work, and he and his wife lived happily for the rest of their lives.

The Little Red Hen

Once upon a time there were three friends, a Rooster, a Mouse and a Little Red Hen. They all lived together in a neat white house on a hill. The Little Red Hen did the cooking and cleaning, and kept everything as bright as a new pin.

At the bottom of the hill and across the stream there was a tumbledown house with peeling paint and dirty windows. A mother fox lived there with her four little foxes. They were always hungry.

One morning the mother fox said to her four little foxes, "I am going out to get some food. Put the pot on to boil, and lay the table ready for supper."

She picked up a dirty old sack, shut the door behind her and set off across the stream and up the hill to the neat white house where the Rooster, the Mouse, and the Little Red Hen lived.

In the kitchen, the Little Red Hen was bustling about getting breakfast.

"Who'll fetch some sticks for the fire?" asked the Little Red Hen.

"I won't," said the Rooster.

"I won't," said the Mouse.

"Then I'll fetch them myself," she said. And she ran and got the sticks and made a roaring fire.

"Who'll fetch some water from the spring?" asked the Little Red Hen.

"I won't," said the Rooster.

"I won't," said the Mouse.

"Then I'll fetch it myself," she said. And she ran to the spring to fill the kettle.

The Little Red Hen made the breakfast and washed the dishes while the Rooster and the Mouse sat and grumbled.

Then the Little Red Hen asked, "Who'll make the beds?"

"I won't," said the Rooster.

"I won't," said the Mouse.

"Then I'll make them myself," said the Little Red Hen, and she bustled away up the stairs, while the Rooster and the Mouse settled themselves in nice cozy armchairs to take a nap.

They were woken by a loud rat-tat-tat at the door.

"Who can that be? Little Red Hen should be here to answer the door," said the Mouse.

"Well, I'm not answering it. I'm too comfortable," said the Rooster.

The Mouse opened the door and the Fox sprang inside.

"Cock-a-doodle-do!" crowed the Rooster as he flew onto the back of the armchair.

"Oh, my! Oh, my!" squeaked the Mouse as she tried to run up the chimney.

But the Fox snatched the Mouse by the tail and pushed her into her sack, and she grabbed the Rooster by the neck and stuffed him into the sack too.

Then the Little Red Hen came running downstairs to see what all the noise was about. As soon as the Fox saw her, she popped the Little Red Hen into the sack too.

Then she tied the sack tightly, threw it over her shoulder and set off down the hill. Poor

Rooster! Poor Mouse! Poor Little Red Hen!

"I wish I hadn't been so grouchy," said the Rooster.

"I wish I hadn't been so lazy," said the Mouse.

"Never mind, I'll think of something," said the Little Red Hen.

By this time the Fox was feeling tired. So she dumped the sack on the ground, lay down under a tree and fell fast asleep.

"Now we can get out!" whispered the Little Red Hen when she heard the Fox's snore.

She took a little pair of scissors out of her apron pocket and snipped a hole in the sacking. The Rooster, the Mouse and the Little Red Hen scrambled out through the hole.

"Now we must find three stones to put in the sack," said the Little Red Hen.

And they did. They rolled three heavy stones up to the sack and pushed them inside through the hole. Then the Little Red Hen got her needle and thread out of her apron pocket and sewed up the hole.

The Rooster, the Mouse and the Little Red Hen ran all the way home to their neat white house as fast as their legs would carry them. They slammed and locked the door and closed all the shutters, and then they felt safe again.

The Fox woke up just as the sun was setting. She slung the sack over her shoulder and set off again.

"This sack feels heavier than ever. The four

little foxes will have a wonderful supper tonight," said the Fox.

But, as she took the first step across the stream, she sank up to her waist. She took a second step, and sank right to the bottom. So the four little foxes didn't get their supper that night after all.

As for the Rooster and the Mouse, they were never lazy or bad-tempered again. The Little Red Hen enjoyed a well-earned rest while the Rooster and the Mouse did all the work, and they all lived happily together for the rest of their lives.

The Musicians of Bremen

Once upon a time there was a donkey who worked hard for his master all his life, carrying sacks of corn to the mill.

One day the donkey's master said to him, "I'll have to get rid of you. You're too old and slow to be useful anymore."

This made the donkey very unhappy. Then he said to himself, "I can still bray beautifully. The other donkeys often say what a fine voice I have. I shall go to Bremen and sing with the town band."

So he trot-trotted down the road to Bremen.

He had not gone very far before he met a dog. The dog was lying by the roadside, barking.

"Why are you barking like that?" asked the donkey.

"My master has thrown me out," said the dog. "He says I'm too old to herd the sheep anymore."

"Why don't you come to Bremen with me?" said the donkey. "You can bark and I can bray and together we can join the town band."

"I'd like that," said the dog, and he wagged his tail.

So the donkey trot-trotted and the dog patter-patted along the road to Bremen.

Before long they met a cat sitting on a wall, meowing.

"Why are you meowing like that?" asked the donkey.

"My mistress has sent me away," said the cat. "She says I'm too old to catch mice."

"Why don't you come to Bremen with us?" said the donkey. "You can meow, the dog can bark, I can bray, and together we can join the town band."

"I'd like that," said the cat.

So the donkey trot-trotted, the dog patter-patted and the cat pad-padded along the road to Bremen.

After a while they came to a farm where a rooster was sitting on a gatepost. He was crowing with all his might.

"Why are you crowing so loudly?" asked the donkey.

There the rooster flew at him, flapping his wings in the robber's face and screeching in his ears.

And the fierce robber ran back into the forest, and was never seen again.

So the donkey, the dog, the cat and the rooster were left in peace. The farmhouse suited them so well that they stayed there and lived happily together. And they never did go and sing with the Bremen town band.

Country Mouse and Town Mouse

There was once a country mouse who lived in a little house under the hedgerow. Every day he swept his house clean and went out into the fields to find seeds and nuts and fruits for his larder. He worked hard, but he was happy for he had everything he needed.

One day Country Mouse's cousin from the town came to stay. Country Mouse was so pleased to see Town Mouse that he made her a

Country Mouse began to think he would never see his little house under the hedgerow again.

Then he heard Town Mouse call out in a loud whisper, "Over here, cousin. Make a run for it!"

Country Mouse climbed down from the table and shot across the floor to Town Mouse. Together they squeezed through the nearest hole in the floorboards.

Country Mouse was trembling all over, but Town Mouse just laughed. "Don't worry," she said, "I'll make sure you get a good meal tomorrow."

That night Country Mouse curled up on Town Mouse's feather bed. He lay awake all night, listening to the cat meowing outside the mousehole.

Next day Country Mouse said to Town Mouse, "It was very kind of you to show me your home, but I really must be going."

"You can't leave before you have a proper meal," said Town Mouse. "Besides, there's so much to see in the town."

"I think I've seen enough, thank you," said Country Mouse.

And with a quick good-bye, he scampered back to the hole in the wall and ran through the town and all the way home.

And from that day onwards he stayed in his little house under the hedgerow, and never dreamed of living in the town again.

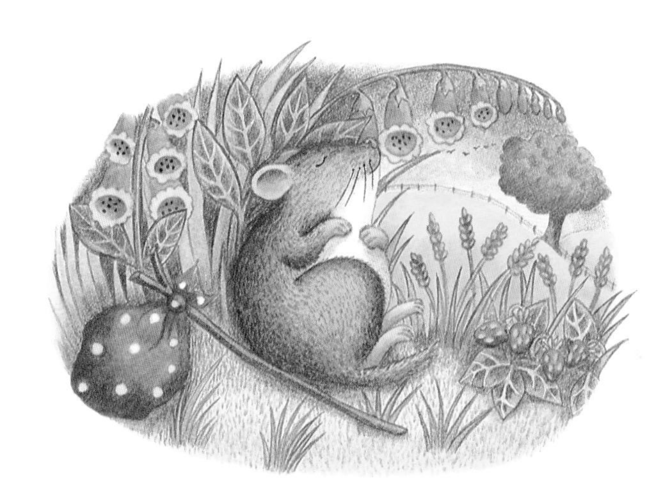

The Three Billy Goats Gruff

Once upon a time there were three billy goats called Big Billy Goat Gruff, Little Billy Goat Gruff and Baby Billy Goat Gruff.

They lived on a rocky hillside where they had only dry grass and thistles to eat. On the hill on the other side of the valley the grass was lush and juicy, and the three billy goats longed to taste it.

But to get to the other side of the valley, the billy goats had to cross a bridge over the stream.

Underneath this bridge lived a big ugly troll, and the billy goats were frightened of him.

One day Baby Billy Goat Gruff said, "I'm hungry!"

Little Billy Goat Gruff said, "I'm hungry too. If only we could get to that luscious grass on the other side of the valley!"

And Big Billy Goat Gruff said, "We must find a way to cross the bridge safely. I will think of a plan." And he did.

Next day Baby Billy Goat Gruff trotted down to the stream. Trip, trap, trip, trap, went his hooves on the bridge.

"Who's that?" bellowed the troll.

"It's only me," said Baby Billy Goat Gruff.

"I'll gobble you up if you cross the bridge," said the troll.

"Please don't. I'm so small that I won't be good to eat," said Baby Billy Goat Gruff. He was trying to be brave but really his legs were trembling. "Why don't you wait until my big brother comes along? He's plumper than I am."

"Oh, all right then," said the troll. "Be off with you."

So Baby Billy Goat Gruff crossed the bridge and ran up the hillside to eat the juicy grass.

Then Little Billy Goat Gruff came down to the stream. Trip, trap, trip, trap, went his hooves on the bridge.

"Who's that?" bellowed the troll.

"It's only me!" said Little Billy Goat Gruff.

"I'll gobble you up if you cross the bridge," said the troll.

"Please don't. I'm not very big, and I won't be good to eat," said Little Billy Goat Gruff with a shiver of fright. "Why don't you wait until my big brother comes along? He'll be nice and tasty."

"Oh, all right then," said the troll. "Be off with you."

So Little Billy Goat Gruff crossed the bridge and ran up the hillside to join his baby brother.

Then along came Big Billy Goat Gruff. Now he really was *very* big, with strong sturdy legs and long curving horns.

When *he* crossed the bridge it creaked and groaned at every step.

"Who's that who dares to cross my bridge?" roared the troll.

"It's me!" said Big Billy Goat Gruff.

"Then I'm coming to gobble you up," said the troll, and he sprang out onto the bridge.

What a horrible fearsome-looking creature he was! But Big Billy Goat Gruff wasn't a bit afraid.

"Oh, you are, are you," he said. "We'll just see about that."

And putting his head down low, he charged at the troll and butted him hard. SPLASH! went the troll as he fell into the stream, and that was the end of him.

So Big Billy Goat Gruff went trip, trap, trip, trap across the bridge and ran up the hillside to join his brothers. And they have lived there from that day to this, enjoying the lush, juicy grass.

Teeny-Tiny

Once upon a time there was a teeny-tiny woman who lived in a teeny-tiny house in a teeny-tiny village.

One day she put on her bonnet and went out for a walk. And when the teeny-tiny woman had gone a teeny-tiny way, she came to a teeny-tiny gate. She opened the teeny-tiny gate and went into a teeny-tiny churchyard.

And when the teeny-tiny woman had gone into the teeny-tiny churchyard, she saw a teeny-tiny bone on a teeny-tiny grave. And the teeny-tiny woman said, "This teeny-tiny bone will make a teeny-tiny bowl of soup for my supper."

So the teeny-tiny woman put the teeny-tiny bone into her teeny-tiny pocket, and went back to her teeny-tiny house.

Now, when she got home, she was a bit tired. So she went upstairs to her teeny-tiny bed and put the teeny-tiny bone into a teeny-tiny cupboard.

Then the teeny-tiny woman got into bed, and went to sleep. She was woken by a teeny-tiny voice from the teeny-tiny cupboard, which said:

"Give me my bone!"

The teeny-tiny woman was a teeny-tiny bit frightened, so she hid her head under the bedcovers and went to sleep again.

Then the teeny-tiny voice cried out a teeny-tiny bit louder:

"Give me my bone!"

This made the teeny-tiny woman a teeny-tiny bit more frightened, so she hid her head a teeny-tiny bit further under the bedcovers.

Then the teeny-tiny voice cried out again a teeny-tiny bit louder still, and it said:

"Give me my bone!"

And this time the teeny-tiny woman put her head out from under the bedcovers and said in her loudest voice:

"TAKE IT!"

The Little Porridge Pot

There was once a little girl who lived with her mother in a little house on the edge of a village. They were very poor and the day came when they had nothing left to eat.

So the mother sent the little girl out into the forest to pick berries. She hadn't gone very far when she met an old woman.

"You look hungry, little girl," said the old woman.

"Oh, I am," said the little girl. "My mother and

I have no food left at home and no money to buy any."

"I can help you," said the old woman, and she took a little cooking pot from her bag. "Take this pot, my dear. And when you say to it, 'Cook, little pot, cook,' it will hiss and bubble and fill with steaming hot porridge. And when you have enough, you can say, 'Stop, little pot, stop.' Then it will stop cooking."

"Oh, thank you," said the little girl and she ran all the way home to her mother. Her mother put the pot on the stove right away.

"Cook, little pot, cook," said the little girl. And at once the pot began to hiss and bubble and to fill with steaming hot porridge.

The little girl and her mother sat down and ate and ate until they could eat no more. Then the little girl said, "Stop, little pot, stop," and the pot stopped cooking.

The little girl and her mother danced around the table for joy, for they knew they would never go hungry again.

pulled. But the turnip didn't budge, no, not one bit.

So the little old man shouted to his wife.

The little old woman pulled the little old man, and the little old man pulled the turnip. But still the turnip didn't budge, no, not one bit.

So the little old woman went next door to fetch the little girl who lived there.

The little girl pulled the little old woman, the little old woman pulled the little old man, and the little old man pulled the turnip. But still the turnip didn't budge, no, not one bit.

So the little girl ran to fetch her brother.

And the little boy pulled the little girl, the little girl pulled the little old woman, the little old woman pulled the little old man, and the little old man pulled the turnip. But still the turnip didn't budge, no, not one bit.

So the little boy whistled for his dog.

The dog pulled the little boy, the little boy pulled the little girl, the little girl pulled the little old woman, the little old woman pulled the little

old man, and the little old man pulled the turnip. But still the turnip didn't budge, no, not one bit.

So the dog barked for the cat.

The cat pulled the dog, the dog pulled the little boy, the little boy pulled the little girl, the little girl pulled the little old woman, the little old woman pulled the little old man, and the little old man pulled the turnip. But still the turnip didn't budge, no, not one bit.

So the cat meowed for the mouse.

And the mouse pulled the cat, the cat pulled the dog, the dog pulled the little boy, the little

boy pulled the little girl, the little girl pulled the little old woman, the little old woman pulled the little old man, and the little old man pulled the turnip.

The earth cracked, the ground gave way and out came the enormous turnip . . . at last!

The little old woman cooked an enormous turnip stew for supper, and the mouse, the cat, the dog, the little boy, the little girl, the little old woman and the little old man all sat down together to eat it. And it was the tastiest meal they ever had in their lives.

The Hedgehog and the Hare

There was once a hedgehog who lived with his wife near a field of cabbages and turnips.

One summer morning, Hedgehog decided to go for a walk to see how his turnips were doing.

He trundled up the path to the turnip field, where he was surprised to see a hare nibbling at his cabbages. But Hare thought the field belonged to him and that the cabbages were *his*.

Hedgehog was a friendly creature and said,

"Good morning, Hare. What a lovely day."

But Hare took not the slightest notice. He just went on eating.

"I thought I'd have a walk before breakfast, to see how my turnips are doing," said Hedgehog.

"A walk before breakfast!" said Hare scornfully. "You won't get far with those short legs."

Hedgehog was hurt by this. He knew his legs were short but they always took him wherever he wanted to go. So he said, "You can be unkind about my legs if you like, but I bet if we ran a race I'd win it."

"You, run faster than me! No one runs faster

than I do," said Hare. "I tell you what – we'll have a race. And then we'll see how well you can run. And if you beat me, you can have my golden coin and my flask of cider."

"All right," said Hedgehog. "But I must go home for my breakfast first. I'll meet you at the far end of the field in half an hour."

Now Hedgehog was sharper-witted than Hare. He had already thought of a way of winning the race.

He went home and told his wife his plan. "You must hide at the finishing post and pop up when you see Hare coming. He will think that you are me and that I have won the race. And won't he be angry!"

usual the ugly duckling was at the very back and was the last to waddle out of the water.

As soon as the other ducks saw him, they started picking on him.

"What's this ugly creature?" said one of the drakes, giving him a sharp poke.

"You can't possibly be a duck," said another.

"I am a duck! I am!" cried the ugly duckling. And he ran away and hid in some reeds, so that none of the other ducks could laugh at him.

Soon it grew dark. The ugly duckling wanted his mother, but he couldn't see where she had

gone. He wandered around on the side of the lake, unable to find his way home. Feeling very small and lonely, he curled up and went to sleep. How he wished he were back home with his mother, even if all the others did make fun of him!

The next morning, as the ugly duckling dabbled around in the water looking for food, two wild ducks flew up.

"What kind of bird are you?" asked one.

"I'm a duck," said the ugly duckling.

"What a funny-looking duck!" said one wild duck to the other.

So the ugly duckling ran away from the wild ducks, stumbling across marshes, over fields, through meadows, until he came to another lake.

"Then I'll come with you," said Cocky Locky.

So Henny Penny and Cocky Locky went to tell the king the sky was falling. They hurried along until they met Ducky Lucky.

"Where are you going, Henny Penny and Cocky Locky?" asked Ducky Lucky.

"We're going to tell the king the sky is falling," said Henny Penny and Cocky Locky.

"Then I'll come with you," said Ducky Lucky.

So Henny Penny, Cocky Locky and Ducky Lucky went to tell the king the sky was falling. They hurried along until they met Goosey Loosey.

"Where are you going, Henny Penny, Cocky Locky and Ducky Lucky?" asked Goosey Loosey.

"We're going to tell the king the sky is falling," said Henny Penny, Cocky Locky and Ducky Lucky.

"Then I'll come with you," said Goosey Loosey.

So Henny Penny, Cocky Locky, Ducky Lucky

and Goosey Loosey went to tell the king the sky was falling. They hurried along until they met Turkey Lurkey.

"Where are you going, Henny Penny, Cocky Locky, Ducky Lucky and Goosey Loosey?" asked Turkey Lurkey.

"We're going to tell the king the sky is falling," said Henny Penny, Cocky Locky, Ducky Lucky and Goosey Loosey.

"Then I'll come with you," said Turkey Lurkey.